NORMAN BRIDWELL

Clifford,
WE LOVE YOU

P9-CCI-106

IT'S CLIFFORD!

SCHOLASTIC INC.
New York   Toronto   London   Auckland   Sydney

To Mira and Usha McClelland

ISBN 0-590-43843-3

Copyright © 1991 by Norman Bridwell.
All rights reserved. Published by Scholastic Inc.
CLIFFORD and CLIFFORD THE BIG RED DOG are
registered trademarks of Norman Bridwell.

It's Clifford music and lyrics by Maureen Lee with appreciation
to Don Zeitler.

36 35 34 33 32 31 30 29   0 1 2/0

Printed in the U.S.A.   24

First Scholastic printing, January 1991

lifford was feeling down-in-the-dumps.

didn't know what to do.

tried everything to cheer him up.

I served his favorite foods.
He wouldn't touch them.

He howled all night long,
for no reason at all.

He didn't even feel like playing with me.

The vet couldn't find anything wrong with Clifford. She said he was just feeling blue.

My friend Alison thought some pretty flowers
might cheer Clifford up.

They didn't.

Clifford loves parades. The kids in the neighborhood
put on a parade for him.

He felt worse than ever. Bill and Marcia said
they would cheer him up with a puppet show.

The show was very good.
He liked it, but then...

...when the witch tried to push the girl
and boy into the oven,

Clifford got upset.

I had an idea. I decided to write a
happy song for Clifford.

I thought of words that say all the wonderful things about
Clifford. I put the words to a tune.

We sang my song to Clifford.
This is how it goes...

Who's the biggest dog around?
Who's the reddest dog in town?

Emily Elizabeth loved that pup...
Loved him so that he grew up.

It's Clifford! It's Clifford!
Lovable, laughable Clifford!
It's Clifford! It's Clifford!
Good old Clifford—yeah! The Big Red Dog!

Who can be a scary ghost?
Who do children love the most?

Who takes Emily for a ride?
Who is always by her side?

It's Clifford! It's Clifford!

Lovable, laughable Clifford!

It's Clifford! It's Clifford!

Good old Clifford—yeah! The Big Red Dog!

Who waits for Emily after school?
Who takes a bath in a swimming pool?

Who tries always to be good?
Who once starred in Hollywood?

It's Clifford! It's Clifford!
Lovable, laughable Clifford!
It's Clifford! It's Clifford!
Good old Clifford—yeah! The Big Red Dog!

Who is Emily's Valentine?
Who makes every day so fine?

Every day they have a ball.
He's the best (WOOF!) dog of all.

It's Clifford! It's Clifford!
Lovable, laughable Clifford!
It's Clifford! It's Clifford!
Good old Clifford—yeah! The Big Red Dog!

The song made Clifford feel much better.
Maybe you would like to sing it, too?

IT'S CLIFFORD!

words and music by Maureen Le

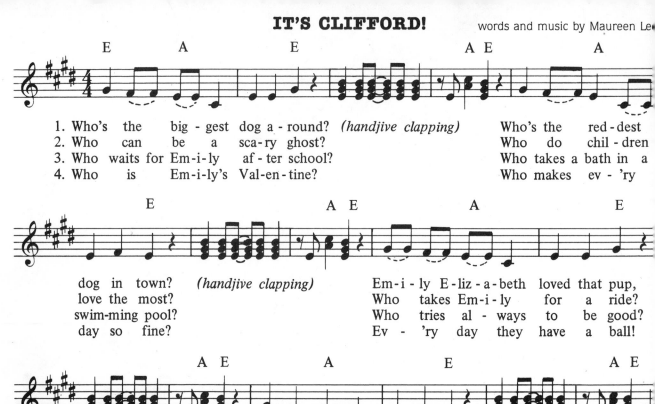

1. Who's the big-gest dog a-round? *(handjive clapping)* Who's the red-dest
2. Who can be a sca-ry ghost? Who do chil-dren
3. Who waits for Em-i-ly af-ter school? Who takes a bath in a
4. Who is Em-i-ly's Val-en-tine? Who makes ev-'ry

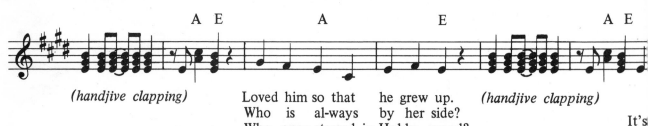

dog in town? *(handjive clapping)* Em-i-ly E-liz-a-beth loved that pup,
love the most? Who takes Em-i-ly for a ride?
swim-ming pool? Who tries al-ways to be good?
day so fine? Ev-'ry day they have a ball!

(handjive clapping) Loved him so that he grew up. *(handjive clapping)*
Who is al-ways by her side?
Who once starred in Hol-ly wood? It's
He's the best (WOOF!) dog of all!

Clif-ford (It's Clif-ford!) Lov-a-ble, laugh-a-ble Clif-ford! It's Clif-ford! (It's

Clif-ford!) Good old Clif-ford-yeah! The Big Red Dog!
(Can be spoken.)